10688
Rinaldo, the Sly Fox

Ursel Scheffler
AR B.L.: 4.1
Points: 0.5

D1004870

Scheuerman School Library
Garden City, KS

A NORTH-SOUTH PAPERBACK

Critical praise for
Rinaldo, the Sly Fox

"In the crime spree that is this easy chapter book's focus, the . . . villain is part rogue, part gentleman-bandit, part duty-shirking Tom Sawyer. . . . But for dissecting the criminal mind, none is better than Bruno, the Duck Detective; and when the two old enemies finally face, readers will be in a fine fettle trying to determine just who won. . . . Those just mastering reading will light into this funny adventure, which pays homage to the clichés of the suspense genre as easily as it parodies them."

Kirkus

Rinaldo, the Sly Fox

by Ursel Scheffler

PICTURES BY
Iskender Gider

TRANSLATED BY
J. Alison James

North-South Books

NEW YORK

Scheuerman School Library
Garden City, KS

Copyright © 1992 by Nord-Süd Verlag AG, Gossau Zürich, Switzerland
First published in Switzerland under the title *Der schlaue Fuchs Rinaldo*
English translation copyright © 1992 by North-South Books Inc.

All rights reserved.
No part of this book may be reproduced or utilized in any form
or by any means, electronic or mechanical, including photocopying,
recording, or any information storage and retrieval system,
without permission in writing from the publisher.

First published in the United States, Great Britain, Canada,
Australia and New Zealand in 1992 by North-South Books,
an imprint of Nord-Süd Verlag AG, Gossau Zürich, Switzerland.
First paperback edition published in 1994.

Distributed in the United States by North-South Books Inc., New York.

Library of Congress Cataloging-in-Publication Data
Scheffler, Ursel.
[Schlaue Fuchs Rinaldo. English]
Rinaldo, the sly fox / by Ursel Scheffler ; pictures by Iskender Gider ;
translated by J. Alison James.
Translation of: Der schlaue Fuchs Rinaldo.
Summary: Rinaldo, the sly fox, tricks everyone but Bruno, the duck detective.
[1. Foxes—Fiction. 2. Animals—Fiction.] I. Gider, Isdender, ill. II. Title.
PZ7.S3425Ri 1992
[E]—dc20 92-2376

British Library Cataloguing in Publication Data
Scheffler, Ursel
Rinaldo the Sly Fox
I. Title II. Gider, Iskender III. James, Alison J.
843.914[J]

ISBN 1-55858-181-2 (TRADE BINDING)
1 3 5 7 9 TB 10 8 6 4 2
ISBN 1-55858-182-0 (LIBRARY BINDING)
1 3 5 7 9 LB 10 8 6 4 2
ISBN 1-55858-359-9 (PAPERBACK)
1 3 5 7 9 PB 10 8 6 4 2

Printed in Belgium

Contents

Rinaldo, the Sly Fox, Makes a Narrow Escape

After Rinaldo, the Sly Fox, stole a goose, a Wanted poster hung on all the trees in Feathertown.

"They'll never catch me," he thought.

But he underestimated Bruno, the Duck Detective. Bruno watched like a hawk to make sure all the local poultry could sleep in peace.

So when Rinaldo came sneaking around again one night, he was surprised by a voice bellowing: "Get your paws up, or I'll shoot!"

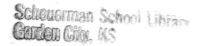
Scheuerman School Library
Garden City, KS

Confound it, Bruno the Duck was on the look-out. This was something Rinaldo had not expected. He squinted into the glare of a bright light and saw he was looking down the big black barrel of a gun.

Shocked, the Fox flipped over backwards and started running.

"Stop right there!" warned Bruno, as he brandished his peashooter.

But Rinaldo didn't stop. Bruno fired a
thundering barrelfull of peas right toward
Rinaldo's backside.

"That was a close one!" gasped Rinaldo
when he reached the edge of the forest. He
threw a last glance back at the friendly town
before he disappeared into the darkness.
"What a real shame," he thought. "I liked
that town. But it would probably be a wise
idea to find a new place to live."

Rinaldo Takes the Fast Train to Paradise

At the other side of the great woods, Rinaldo found train tracks. He ran alongside the tracks until he reached a station. In the grey light of early morning, he boarded a train and took it south for many hours.

When the train stopped in Zoo City, Rinaldo helped himself to a coat and sunglasses from a sleeping passenger and got off. He pulled up the coat collar, put on the sunglasses.

Rinaldo's stomach growled. He desperately needed a good meal. But he'd spent his last penny on the train ticket. There wasn't even any money in the stolen coat. Still, Rinaldo was not worried. He was used to finding meals without having to pay for them.

Rinaldo walked over to the station master. The Cat was busy opening the gate on the road which crossed the tracks.

"Excuse me," said Rinaldo politely. "Could you recommend a good hotel?"

"But of course! Paradise is just around the corner!" said the Cat, laughing.

"Paradise?" asked Rinaldo, confused.

"The Paradise *Hotel*, of course! Famous for its fine food."

"Then that is the place for me," said the Fox, and he went on his way.

A friendly Pig stood at the entrance to the hotel. When he saw the Fox, he pulled the door open and said, "Welcome to Paradise!"

"Thank you very much," said Rinaldo, and he swaggered into the hotel lobby as if he were King of the Forest himself.

The receptionist was impressed. "Our finest room is available for you," he said, "number 303. If you would please sign your name and address in our guest book."

He handed the new guest the room key. It was hanging on a golden apple.

"I realize it is nearly three o'clock," said Rinaldo as he wrote a false name in the guest book. "But is it still possible to get a bite to eat?"

"Absolutely," said the Badger. "The dining room is just through that glass door."

The Fox went into the dining room and
found the largest table. His mouth started to
water as soon as he picked up the menu.

He ordered three main courses and five desserts. "Food always tastes better when it's on the house," he chuckled to himself.

"Put everything on the bill for room 303," he said. Then he went up to his room to take a nap.

On the stairway, he met a lovely Hen who jangled with expensive jewelry.

"She looks like the Hen who laid the golden egg," thought Rinaldo, and he smiled. It would certainly pay to meet her. But right now he was too tired, so he merely gave the Hen a dazzling smile.

Within minutes, Rinaldo was snoring atop down pillows in a heavenly bed in the finest room of the Paradise Hotel, dreaming of a tree filled with golden apples.

Rinaldo Charms
a Foolish Hen

It was already dark when Rinaldo woke up. His throat was dry from snoring, and he was terribly thirsty.

He splashed the sleep from his eyes with some cold water. Now he could think clearly again: First he had to get himself something to drink. Then he would be ready for a little excitement. He decided to go down and take a look around the hotel. The last guests were just coming from dinner. In the lounge he spotted a group of admirers crowding around that picture-perfect Hen!

"May I?" asked the Fox, pointing at a free seat.

"By all means. You seem to be quite a nice fellow," said the Hen. She moved over to make some room for him.

A Pony from Texas was just telling tales about his home, where everything was much bigger, more beautiful, and much more fun than anywhere else in the world.

"Show off," grumbled the Rhino. He came from a town in the north. He was spending his two week holiday in Zoo City, because of the famous mineral baths.

The Mountain Goat told an extremely long joke that everyone already knew. The lovely Hen laughed anyway. She gave a throaty chuckle and spilled her juice.

The Duck in the striped shirt said: "It is certainly more practical when one wears stripes. The only stains which show on me are chocolate."

It was an altogether pleasant evening. At the end the Fox stood up and called for the waiter.

"The drinks are on me," said the Fox. "Just put it on the tab for room 303!"

"Oh thank you so much," said the Goat.

"How generous!" quacked the Duck.

"Merci," said the well-educated Rhino.

"It just goes to prove that there still are gentlemen," clucked the Hen. She had not yet noticed that her pearl necklace was missing.

Rinaldo Leaves
Paradise Without Paying

The next morning Rinaldo was up with
the sun. He ran to the nearest phone booth
and sent himself a telegram at the Paradise
Hotel. It arrived when he was at breakfast.
The Fox read it and pretended to be amazed.

"I am terribly sorry," he said to the receptionist. "I have to leave immediately. Could you please get my bill ready?" The Badger was still a little sleepy when he handed the Fox his bill.

"Oh, dear. This is a bit higher than I was expecting. I don't have this much cash on hand. Would it be possible for you to send the bill to my home?" asked the Fox.

"No problem," said the Badger. "Your address is here in the guest book: 4 Peapod Street, Feathertown. Did I read that correctly without my glasses?"

"Exactly right," said Rinaldo.

Hastily he gathered his things, since he heard excited squawking and quacking coming from the stairs. "I must hurry," said Rinaldo as he dashed out the front door. "My train is leaving in just a few minutes!"

"Have a good trip," called the friendly Pig.

Bruno the Duck Gets a Surprise from Paradise

When Bruno the Duck was cooking his oatmeal the next morning, he looked out of the kitchen window. There was the postman, waving at him with a letter.

Bruno dropped his spoon and ran to the garden gate. His heart was beating fast, because he was expecting a letter from his girlfriend.

His heart beat even faster after he had ripped open the letter.

It was no letter! It was a bill. A bill from the Paradise Hotel.

"This is ridiculous! I have never even been to this hotel!" Bruno ran to the telephone. He explained to the bewildered Badger that there had been a terrible mistake.

The Badger was shocked. "Then the Fox was an impostor!"

"Did you say Fox? There is only one Fox sly enough to pull off a caper like this: Rinaldo! I am a detective. I will take on this case myself!" promised Bruno, and he slammed down his phone.

"Just you wait, Rinaldo, you scoundrel," he hissed. Under his white feathers, his skin got purple goose bumps, he was so furious. "I'm going to get you this time!"

He buckled on his pea shooter and set out to stop the crook in his tracks. A friend who was a pilot flew him to Zoo City. They landed in a meadow, and Bruno immediately started his investigation.

"A very daaaangerous fellow! I could tell that immediately."

"My necklace is gone! The thief! The impostor!"

"He went to the railroad station, because he was taking the next train."

How Rinaldo
Gets a New Sports Car

Of course Rinaldo did not go to the railroad station. He ran in the opposite direction. Within five minutes, he had disappeared into a thick forest. He cut through the underbrush, enjoying the run. He was well rested, well fed and happy. After a couple of hours, he could hear the sound of a highway in the distance.

"I think I will get myself a car," he decided. "Then I can make my getaway without leaving tracks!"

Rinaldo ran along to the nearest rest area.
He had already worked out how he would
get a car. He just needed to find someone
who was stupid enough to fall for his trick.

The Fox carefully watched all the cars and
their drivers. Most of the drivers only parked
for a moment, went into the service station
and drove out again.

Finally the right victim came along. A Weasel zoomed in, driving a flashy gold convertible sports car. The Fox's mouth watered. This fellow had good taste in cars!

As Rinaldo watched, the Weasel got out. He left the top down and went off to find the toilet.

The Weasel was back in a minute, and he jumped into his car. But when he turned the key, the engine wouldn't start.

He tried again and again to start the car, but it was useless. Just then Rinaldo came sauntering by.

"May I help you? My name is René. I am a car mechanic," he said.

"Pardon me? Oh yes!" said the Weasel, delighted. "Car mechanic? This is a stroke of luck. I would be very grateful if you could get this baby moving again."

"If you'll just stay at the wheel, I'll be happy to give you a push," said the Fox.

The Weasel sat in the driver's seat.

The Fox pushed.

The ignition gave a short cough, but the car didn't start.

This was no great surprise to Rinaldo, since he had disconnected a coil wire.

"Just a minute," said the Fox, acting very businesslike. "Could I take a look at the engine? I drive a car just like this, only green. Mine does the same thing sometimes."

Rinaldo fiddled around a while and then said: "The engine is flooded. You have to have just the right touch to get it started when it's like this. If you like, I could give it a try myself."

40

Scheuerman School Library
Garden City, KS

The Weasel happily agreed. He was in a hurry. The sooner the car was going the better.

The Fox sat down in the driver's seat.

"You'll need to give me a little push," he said. "Can you manage that?"

"Sure, of course!" declared the Weasel. "I'm in better shape than I look."

He shoved up his jacket sleeves and started to push. While Rinaldo leaned back comfortably in the soft seat, the Weasel dripped with sweat.

When the car was going at a good pace, the Fox turned the key. The engine started at once. He put his foot down, and the car roared away.

The Weasel was left at the side of the road feeling very bewildered. It took a little while before he realized that he had helped a thief steal his own car.

Rinaldo Settles Down to Life on a Farm

Feeling wonderful, Rinaldo drove his new sports car through the countryside. After a few hours, he heard on the radio that the police were looking for the Weasel's stolen car and gave his plate number. He decided it would be a good idea to get off the highway for a while.

Along a little country road, Rinaldo saw a sign that made him hungry: Good Food.

He put on the brakes and found himself a parking place.

The waitress welcomed Rinaldo. She recommended the noodle soup with wild mushrooms. Rinaldo ordered a bowl.

When he was full, he looked thoughtfully out of the window. This was a nice area. A river, woods, and gentle hills. There were even mountain peaks in the distance.

Maybe he should stay here in the country a while, until the grass had grown over certain things.

Rinaldo quietly leafed through the wallet that he had found in the Weasel's car. He was quite satisfied with what he found.

"Tell me something," Rinaldo said to the waitress. "Is it difficult to find an inexpensive little house around here?"

"Well, there is a little place by the corn field down along the river. It belongs to Beaver. He just got married and built a new house. Would you like me to call him?"

The Fox liked the Beaver's place immediately. It was an ideal location. Far enough from the road to have a quiet life and yet close enough to town to have friends, who always came in handy. Besides, it was the right price. It wasn't exactly beautiful—actually it was falling to pieces—but that could be fixed.

With the help of many workers soon the shack became a beautiful country cottage. The Fox sat on a bench and looked out over the field that he now owned.

He imagined tall stalks of golden corn growing there. He thought about the popcorn and corn on the cob, and sacks of cornmeal that he could sell for good money.

Rinaldo Plants a Field of Corn Without Lifting a Paw

When the house was freshly painted and the roof didn't leak, it looked quite good. The corn field, however, looked awful. It was full of weeds. Who would dig the rows and plant the seeds? Unfortunately, the Weasel's wallet was empty by now.

The Fox sat on a stone at the edge of his field and thought. It didn't take long before he had a good idea.

He decided to hold a contest. The one who could dig and plant a row of corn the fastest would win a hundred pieces of gold.

All the animals poured in. Everyone thought that it would be nothing to dig and plant a row. It was as bustling and noisy as the county fair.

First everyone had to buy a shovel for ten gold pieces. They paid it, because no one had remembered to bring their own. Finally they went to the starting line.

There were over a hundred participants, one in every furrow. With a bang, the work began.

Families and friends stood and cheered. And because they got so thirsty from cheering, the Fox sold fresh lemonade.

Start

The winner was a Hamster, the smart little son of the bank manager, who had eaten extra vitamins at breakfast that morning.

Rinaldo was satisfied. He happily paid out the hundred gold pieces because he knew the real winner was himself. He had managed to get all those animals to work for him for nothing, and he had even made a lot of money selling shovels and lemonade.

Rinaldo Snares
a Big Surprise

Rinaldo enjoyed the quiet country life for a while, watching the corn as it grew. But as everyone knows, there is nothing harder to bear than an endless line of perfect days. In any case, one morning the Fox was terribly bored.

54

He thought back on those exciting times, when he would slip into the hen houses at night or follow the waddling geese down to the pond.

He remembered how wonderful it was to outwit Bruno the Duck. That is what he really missed!

"I would really like to snare a goose once more and then roast it for Sunday dinner," thought Rinaldo longingly. Just thinking about it made his mouth water.

Rope snare traps were his specialty. There was no escaping from his rope snare with the special double-trouble slip knot.

That afternoon, Rinaldo slipped into the woods. There, along the small path to the goose pond, he laid out his trap. He covered it with twigs and leaves so it couldn't be seen. He was pleased with his work.

Suddenly a voice bellowed from behind: "Paws up, or I'll shoot!"

Rinaldo jumped up and spun around. In his surprise, he stepped right into his own trap.

"We have a bill to settle, my friend," said
Bruno the Duck in a dangerously quiet
voice.

Rinaldo hung from the tree, squeezed his eyes shut and pretended he was knocked out. But he was thinking fast. He couldn't let himself be captured by the Duck Detective. He had always managed to outsmart Bruno in the past and he wasn't going to give up now. As he dangled from the rope, face to face with his most dangerous foe, he thought of a brilliant way to escape. . . .

About the Author

Ursel Scheffler was born in Nuremberg,
the German city where many toys are made.
She has written over 100 children's books,
which have been published in 15 different
languages. She has a special liking for foxes and
other two- and four-legged tricksters—as you
can see from this story.

About the Illustrator

Iskender Gider was born in Istanbul, Turkey. When he was nine years old, he moved with his parents to Germany, where he went to school in Cologne and Rechlinghausen. Today he is a commercial artist and an assistant professor at the University of Essen. The things he most likes to paint in picture books are elephants, pigs, chickens and foxes—especially sly foxes like Rinaldo.

About the Translator

Alison James is the author of two novels for young adults, *Sing for a Gentle Rain* and *Runa*. She also translates German and Swedish children's books. You'd never guess it, but a sly fox lives in the field behind her house, and she can see him if she is very quiet.